Kiki's Blankie

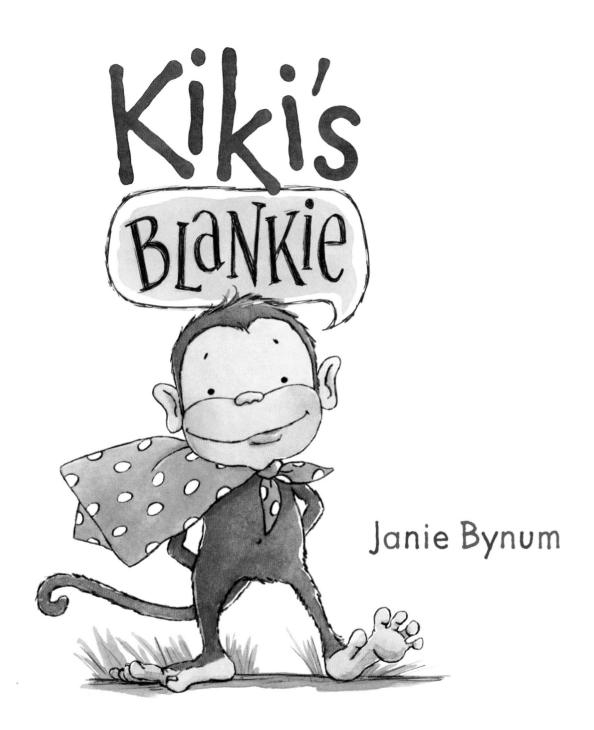

Janie Bynum

STERLING

New York / London

For Taylor.

Thanks for being the loving monkey—
I mean SON—that you are!

STERLING and the distinctive Sterling logo are registered trademarks of Sterling Publishing Co., Inc.

Library of Congress Cataloging-in-Publication Data Available

2 4 6 8 10 9 7 5 3 1

Published by Sterling Publishing Co., Inc.

387 Park Avenue South, New York, NY 10016

Text and illustrations copyright © 2009 by Janie Bynum

Distributed in Canada by Sterling Publishing

c/o Canadian Manda Group, 165 Dufferin Street

Toronto, Ontario, Canada M6K 3H6

Distributed in the United Kingdom by GMC Distribution Services

Castle Place, 166 High Street, Lewes, East Sussex, England BN7 1XU

Distributed in Australia by Capricorn Link (Australia) Pty. Ltd.

P.O. Box 704, Windsor, NSW 2756, Australia

Sterling ISBN 978-1-4027-5910-9

For information about custom editions, special sales, premium
and corporate purchases, please contact Sterling Special Sales
Department at 800-805-5489 or specialsales@sterlingpublishing.com.

The illustrations for this book were created using traditional watercolor and digital media.

Designed by Scott Piehl

This is Kiki.

Kiki adores her
polka-dot blankie.

She never goes
anywhere without it.

Kiki's blankie is a
terrific tent.

And a nifty napkin.

Kiki won't wear anything else.

With her blankie,
Kiki is a pirate.

And a cowgirl.

She's Super Kiki!

One day Kiki goes sailing.

A big wind blows
and Kiki's blankie flies.

Kiki can't sail without her blankie.

Kiki spies her blankie
flapping in the breeze.

She runs to snatch it
from a branch.

But below the branch,
a huge crocodile sleeps!

Kiki imagines scaring
the beast away.

But she isn't very scary
without her blankie.

Kiki thinks about flying
over the crocodile.

But she isn't Super Kiki
without her blankie.

Kiki imagines her
blankie being eaten.

Suddenly Kiki feels very brave!

Kiki scampers up a tree.

She swings down and
stretches as far as she can.

A breeze blows and Kiki flies...

…over the bamboo, across
the pond, and home.

When Kiki gets home, she has a bath.
So does her blankie.

Kiki waits. She never goes
anywhere without her blankie...

...even in her dreams.